DRUMS AT SARATOGA

by Lisa Banim

SILVER MOON PRESS

NEW YORK

DRUMS AT SARATOGA
by Lisa Banim
Copyright © 1993 by Kaleidoscope Press

For information contact
Silver Moon Press
New York, New York
(800) 874-3320

Designed by John J. H. Kim
Printed in the United States of America

Library of Congress Cataloging-in-Publication Data

Banim, Lisa, 1960-
    Drums at Saratoga / by Lisa Banim.
    p. cm. -- (Stories of the States)
    Includes bibliographical references
    Summary: Lured by the glamour and excitement of a soldier's life, eleven-year-old Nathaniel follows the British army down the Hudson Valley during the American Revolution and witnesses the true hardships of war firsthand.
    ISBN 1-881889-20-3 (hardcover): $13.95
    ISBN 1-881889-70-X (paperback): $5.95
    1. United States--History--Revolution, 1775-1783--Juvenile fiction. [1. United States--History--Revolution, 1775-1783--Fiction.] I. Title. II. Series.
PZ7.B2253Dr 1993
[Fic]--dc20

93-16460
CIP
AC

STORIES OF THE STATES

TABLE OF CONTENTS

CHAPTER ONE
"A Bold Young Fellow"

"Pull, you lazy good-for-nothing!" Eleven-year-old Nathaniel Phillips shook himself out of his daydream. He tugged hard on the chain beside him. If he didn't keep the bellows going, the forge fire would go out.

Nathaniel had been picturing himself as a soldier in the glorious army of King George. He dreamed of himself in a scarlet coat, white breeches, and tall hat. Nathaniel glanced down at the clothes he actually wore. They were dirty and caked with sweat.

"Pay attention, boy!" Master Rodman called to Nathaniel.

"Yes, sir," Nathaniel mumbled. He pulled on the chain again. If the fire went out, Nathaniel knew he'd receive a severe beating.

Master Rodman reached for his sledgehammer. Then he began to pound white-hot iron into an ax head. Sparks flew through the dark, hot, grimy air.

Nathaniel gazed into the fire. Why had he ever agreed to be Master Rodman's apprentice? Now he was stuck for seven years, learning to be a blacksmith. It was a trade that did not interest him at all.

After his parents had died of the smallpox, Nathaniel had few places to go. He could have gone to work for his sister Polly in New York state. Then he'd be working on a farm, instead of inside a dark, blazing hot forge in Canada. It's too late now, he thought with a sigh.

"Blacksmith!" a voice boomed from the door.

Nathaniel turned around, and Master Rodman lowered his hammer. A man strode into the forge dressed in the pure white breeches and crisp scarlet coat of the British army. Nathaniel gasped. It was as if his daydream itself had walked in. He had seen many such soldiers recently, but never expected actually to meet one. Behind the man was a tall, thin black boy, a few years older than Nathaniel.

"How may I be of service to one of King George's men?" Master Rodman asked, a fawning smile on his face. He hastily wiped his hands on his leather apron.

"General Burgoyne is short of horses," the soldier said. "Would you tell us which good farmers or townspeople might be willing to part with their beasts? We offer a fair price."

Master Rodman shook his head. "I am sorry, sir. But the army has already taken nearly every horse and ox to be found in St. John's."

"I feared as much," the soldier said, shaking his head. "We have but half the horses and oxen needed to carry our men, let alone pull the carts and cannon."

"It's a grand army that's come to St. John's," Nathaniel said eagerly. "Where are you headed?"

Master Rodman glared at Nathaniel. "My apprentice does not appear to know his place," he told the officer.

To Nathaniel's surprise, the soldier reached down and tousled his hair. "A bold young fellow, eh?" he said. "We could use men with your spirit as we march toward Albany."

Nathaniel's heart raced. "My sister Polly lives near there," he told the soldier. "She married an American rebel," he explained, "but my parents were Tories, loyal to the British crown. We came to Canada when the war began. Now I'm ready to return—with the British army!"

Master Rodman looked angrily at Nathaniel, but the soldier laughed. "Well, lad, you're a bit young yet," he said. "Some day soon you can return home in safety. General Burgoyne has promised to end this rebellion by Christmas."

"Oh," Nathaniel said, disappointment in his voice. Would the war end before he had a chance to take part in a battle?

"Perhaps you shouldn't speak of all this in front of the boy," Master Rodman said. "He is something of a troublemaker."

The officer chuckled. "No matter. 'Tis a brilliant plan, you see. At Albany, our troops will join with an army of Tories and Indians from the west. Then both armies will meet up with a huge force of His Majesty's best men heading up the Hudson River from New York. Our three armies will control the Hudson, and the rebel scoundrels will find the northern and southern colonies divided. When that day arrives, my friends, four-and-twenty General Washingtons could not save the American army."

Nathaniel gazed at the soldier in admiration. "If I were old enough, I'd join the British army myself," he said.

The man smiled. "I'm sure you'll make a fine soldier one day. Perhaps we'll meet again. My name is Captain Marshall." Then he turned to Master Rodman. "I'd best be off," he said. "Our expedition begins today. Thank you for your trouble, blacksmith."

Master Rodman nodded. "Godspeed," he said. But as soon as the soldier and his servant had left, the smile faded from Master Rodman's face. He turned and glared at Nathaniel. "I'll teach you to hold your tongue, you impudent boy," he snarled, raising his hand.

At that moment, the midday bells began to toll. Master Rodman stopped. "Dinner time," he muttered, as he removed his leather apron. "Mind the forge while I take my meal," he told Nathaniel curtly. "I'll deal with you later."

The minute Master Rodman had gone, Nathaniel dropped onto a low stool. If only he could join General Burgoyne's army, he thought miserably. He could almost hear the drums and fifes playing, as the great flag of Britain whipped in the June breeze.

Boom!

Nathaniel sat up. The soldiers at the harbor were firing their cannon! Nathaniel strained his ears. He had not been daydreaming after all. In the distance, he actually could hear the fifes and drums of the British army.

He jumped up from the stool and ran to the door of the forge. Nathaniel blinked for a moment as his eyes adjusted to the blinding sunshine. He saw that a great crowd had gathered near the waterfront. Nathaniel heard a band playing, and saw soldiers bidding farewell to loved ones. Regiments of hired German soldiers, Canadians, Tories, and a large group of Indians were preparing to depart with the army.

Without a moment's hesitation, Nathaniel headed for the harbor. When he reached the waterfront, Nathaniel stopped to gaze at the mighty fleet anchored there. The British had the most powerful navy in the world. Nathaniel stared in awe at the huge guns of the vessel *Thunderer.* The boat was moored in the Richelieu River. It would help carry the mighty army south into the rebels' homeland.

At that moment, a great shout arose from the crowd. "'Tis Gentleman Johnny!" a woman near Nathaniel cried, clasping her hands. "General Burgoyne is here!"

Nathaniel turned to see a handsome officer with flashing dark eyes and a jutting jaw ride past on a large brown horse.

The gallant General Burgoyne tipped his hat to the ladies and waved at the crowd. All around Nathaniel people were pushing to get a closer look at Gentleman Johnny. Horses whinnied and pranced skittishly as they were led toward the waiting vessels. Slow, sure-footed oxen passed by, hitched to small wooden carts loaded with cannon and supplies for the army.

The guns of the nearby fort and the British fleet roared out a thunderous salute. The sound echoed off the wooded hillsides and over the quiet waters of the river.

"The rebels will hear 'em coming!" a man shouted.

Just then, Nathaniel felt a painful jab in the back. "Out of my way, boy," a fat, red-faced woman said. She was carrying a large pot, and dragged two dirty-faced children behind her.

Nathaniel stared after the woman, who pushed past him to join a group of women and children. Were they all going with the army? Soldiers' wives and sweethearts often followed the army to cook and launder for the soldiers, he knew. But there were so many of them!

"They'll all be fine enough sailing down the river and along Lake Champlain," an old man beside Nathaniel said, while he puffed his corncob pipe. "But all those carts and camp followers will slow the soldiers down when they have to cut their way through the wilderness."

"Nothing will slow the British army down," Nathaniel told him confidently. The old man grunted and turned away.

Then an idea began to form in Nathaniel's mind. Perhaps he was too young to be a soldier, but why couldn't he be a camp follower? He would be much more helpful than these women and children. And if he were given the chance, Nathaniel was sure he could prove himself brave enough to become a soldier. Here was his chance to take part in glorious battles before the war ended.

The band struck up a lively marching tune, and the crowd cheered again. Nathaniel looked back toward the village and the dark, hot forge where Master Rodman was probably already looking for him.

He had nothing to lose. Nathaniel Phillips, former blacksmith's apprentice, decided to embark on the adventure of his life!

CHAPTER TWO
"The English Never Lose Ground"

Nathaniel sat near the campfire, huddled in a worn, scratchy blanket. It was three months since he had joined General Burgoyne's expedition, and the September night air was cool.

It was quiet around the campfire. Most of the women and children had long since gone to sleep. Over the crackling fire, Nathaniel could hear a soldier's sweetheart giggling. Here and there men's voices were raised in song. This was the part of army life that Nathaniel liked best. The soldiers sat around a campfire and told glorious tales over a dipper of rum.

"We cross the Hudson tomorrow," one of the soldiers was saying. "We'll soon face the Americans on the west bank."

"The rebel cowards will turn and run all the way to Albany, I reckon," another soldier said.

"Leaving more felled trees in the path of our wagons, no doubt," a third soldier said glumly. "It takes us half the day just to clear them."

Captain Marshall, the officer Nathaniel had met in Master Rodman's forge, reached behind him for another bottle of rum. "And what of it?" he asked. "Our troubles will soon be over. Once we've crossed the Hudson and beaten the rebels, we'll travel down the river with ease."

The first soldier chuckled. "And once the

rebels are routed, we'll be enjoying champagne, fine meals, and good company just like Gentleman Johnny there beyond the hill."

A ruddy soldier shook his head. "Perhaps we will not defeat the Americans so easily. I've heard it said that the king has abandoned us. The two armies who were to join us have been sent to other battles."

"Bah, 'tis only a rumor," a heavy man in a powdered wig said. "And anyway, we need no help to wipe out the ragged American army."

"Have you forgotten what happened at Bennington?" the red-faced soldier said bitterly. "Gentleman Johnny sent troops to bring us fresh supplies and horses. Instead, they ran into one of your 'ragged American armies,' and—"

"That's enough!" Captain Marshall snapped.

Nathaniel frowned. He had seen the survivors of the Battle of Bennington, and heard their stories of the terrible defeat. This wasn't the soldiers' talk he liked to hear. Where were the tales of glorious victories the soldiers used to tell? It was too bad he'd been stuck drawing water and polishing boots all these months. He could show these soldiers a thing or two, if only they'd let him fight.

Captain Marshall stood up. "Take heart, men," he said with a sigh. "Even if we meet with no help, 'tis only a matter of time before the rebels are finished." Captain Marshall walked wearily from the campfire, followed by his young servant.

Even if we meet with no help.

The captain's words lingered in Nathaniel's mind. Did Captain Marshall know something the others did not? Were the rumors true? Nathaniel watched while the captain's servant followed him into the tent. If only he could be an officer's servant instead of a mere camp follower, Nathaniel thought with envy. That boy probably got to hear the officers making their battle plans. He must know everything that went on. It wasn't fair, Nathaniel thought. Not fair at all.

NATHANIEL WOKE AT DAWN the next morning. He heard drums in the distance. The advance army was already preparing to cross the river. He quickly rolled out of his blanket and headed to the center of the camp.

Nathaniel gazed in awe as the soldiers formed their ranks. A few minutes before, they had been a mass of sleepy men. Now they stood in straight rows. Their backs were rigid, and their rifles gleamed in the early light. The band struck up *The Grenadier's March*. Suddenly, Nathaniel felt someone grab him by the shoulder.

Nathaniel yelled with surprise as he was pulled to the ground. At that moment, horses thundered by. He realized that he could easily have been trampled. Nathaniel looked up at the person who had saved him. It was Captain Marshall's young servant.

"Thank you," Nathaniel said, scrambling to his feet. "I wasn't paying attention, I guess." He held out his hand. "I'm Nathaniel Phillips. You came into the forge back in St. John's, looking for horses."

The boy nodded and shook Nathaniel's hand. "I remember," he said. "You're the one eager for battle. My name is Ben Freeman."

At that moment the advance troops, led by General Simon Fraser, began to march. The two boys turned to watch the troops parade by. With colors flying and bands playing, the army headed to the river. Nathaniel felt very proud as the line of stiffly stepping soldiers paraded past, the steel of their bayonets glinting in the early morning sun.

As General Fraser and his men reached the river's edge they passed by General Burgoyne. He and his aides sat on horseback, watching the troops go by. General Fraser saluted General Burgoyne smartly and marched on. He led his troops toward a line of boats stretched across the broad river. They had been tied together to form a bridge.

General Burgoyne took his hat from his head and swept it through the air, saluting the troops. "The English never lose ground!" he cried. Nathaniel's ears were filled with the roaring cheers of the soldiers.

Nathaniel turned and smiled at Ben. He saw that the older boy looked troubled.

"What's the matter?" Nathaniel asked, frowning. "Why did you not cheer with everyone else? Our army is crossing the river. Soon we will destroy the rebels."

Ben's eyes did not leave the water. "Once our troops have crossed the river, they will lose all contact with Canada. And no one knows how large an army we will face. Gentleman Johnny has taken a very big gamble," he said, and shook his head. "There will be no turning back now."

CHAPTER THREE
"The Life of the Soldier Is the Property of the King!"

"Fire! Fire!" Nathaniel sat up. Had he been dreaming? "Fire!" someone shouted again.

It was two nights after the army had crossed the Hudson. Nathaniel rubbed his eyes and poked his head out of the tent he shared with several other camp followers.

"What's going on?" he asked a soldier who was running by the tent.

"Major Acland's tent is afire!" the soldier yelled. "Make haste! Help us fill buckets with water."

Nathaniel scrambled to his feet and grabbed a bucket from the ground in front of the tent. He ran toward the river in the darkness. Glancing over his shoulder, he saw a nearby tent engulfed in flames.

Nathaniel now sprinted to the river, dipped his bucket into the water, and headed back up the hill. As he came to the burning tent from behind, Nathaniel saw a woman crawl out from under the flap. She was coughing and groping at the dirt, but seemed unhurt.

Nathaniel ran to the front of the tent. He handed his bucket to a line of men fighting the fire there. Then he saw Major Acland struggle with the soldiers holding him back. "Let me go, man," Acland shouted. "She's in there, I tell you!"

Nathaniel watched with horror as Major

Acland threw off the men who held him. Acland sprinted into the blazing tent.

"Wait, sir!" Nathaniel called. "Lady Acland is safe!" But the major didn't hear. Nathaniel hesitated for a moment, then rushed into the tent after him.

Searing heat hit Nathaniel's face like a wall. He squinted as the hot, black smoke burned his eyes. Coughing and sputtering in the thick smoke, he finally saw the major in front of him. Nathaniel grabbed Acland's night shirt and tried to drag the man out.

"Let go of me, boy!" Major Acland shouted. "I must save my wife!"

"Lady Acland is outside," Nathaniel gasped, choking on the smoke.

The major hesitated. Pieces of flaming canvas dropped near Nathaniel's feet. "Come, sir," Nathaniel urged. "She's safe, I saw her with my own two eyes." He tugged again at Acland's night shirt, then lost his balance. Nathaniel sprawled onto the ground, barely able to breathe.

Major Acland helped Nathaniel to his feet. The two rushed from the blazing tent. As soon as they were back in the cool night air, the burning tent collapsed in a shower of sparks. Nathaniel threw himself to the ground, coughing. He heard a squeal of joy, as Lady Acland ran to her husband. She threw her arms around him and began to sob.

The major turned to Nathaniel, his face covered with soot. "You're a brave lad," he said. "What is your name?"

"Nathaniel Phillips, sir," he replied.

"I owe you my life," Major Acland said.

"'Twas nothing, sir," Nathaniel said.

"Nonsense," Acland replied. "I'll not soon forget what you've done, young Phillips."

Soon the fire was put out. As Major Acland led his wife away, Ben came up beside Nathaniel. "A close call," he said. "How did the blaze start?"

"'Twas the major's dog," a man behind

them said. "He turned over a table on which a candle was burning."

Nathaniel yawned. The excitement was over and he was exhausted. "There's an hour or so till dawn," he said. "I need more sleep."

"That you do," Ben nodded. "The army will be moving again, I think."

Nathaniel dragged himself back to his tent and took up his scratchy blanket. He was lucky to have any covering at all, he told himself, now that the nights were growing cold.

Nathaniel wondered sleepily whether the grand plan to divide and conquer the colonies could possibly fail. No, he quickly assured himself, the English never lose ground.

Just as Nathaniel was dropping off to sleep, he heard an eerie sound. He sat up and his heart raced.

The noise was like a faint, distant scratching. At first, Nathaniel thought some woodland creatures were trying to get into the tent. But when his head cleared, Nathaniel recognized the sound.

It was a drumbeat.

Somewhere near Saratoga the rebels sounded their drums. The enemy waited, unseen.

IT SEEMED TO NATHANIEL that he had hardly closed his eyes when Mistress Dargin, a soldier's wife, was shaking him by the shoulder. 'Tis nearly seven, Nathaniel," she said. "We'll be needing water."

Nathaniel tucked his shirt into his breeches and went outside to fetch a bucket. Some of the other boys were already bringing wood for the fires. Everything in camp seemed normal.

Nathaniel paused. Had he really heard those distant drums at daybreak? Perhaps he had been dreaming.

"General Burgoyne is sure the American camp is not far away from us."

Nathaniel stopped. A pair of soldiers

talked while they pulled on their boots. "Gentlemen Johnny leaves this morning with two thousand men to search for the rebels," the other soldier replied.

Nathaniel scurried down the riverbank. He was definitely going with the soldiers this time, he told himself. No matter what.

When Nathaniel returned to camp with his bucket, he saw a familiar figure seated on a horse.

"Good morning, young Phillips," Major Acland said.

"Good morning, sir," Nathaniel replied.

"I want to thank you again for saving me last night," the major said. "My poor wife was certain she would never see me again. If there is any way I can repay you—"

"There is!" Nathaniel blurted.

Major Acland smiled. "I thought as much," he said. "What is it? New shoes? Fresh clothing?"

"Please, sir," Nathaniel said. "Let me

come along with the troops who are searching for the rebels today." Major Acland threw his head back and laughed.

"This is the first time I've heard anyone beg to join a forced march," he said. "All right. You can be my aide for the day. Come along with the regiment and help me when we break from marching." With that, the British officer spurred his horse and rode away.

Nathaniel was thrilled. Finally, he was to march with the soldiers, not spend the day polishing boots in camp.

Once more, he could almost picture himself in the scarlet uniform of the British army.

"BOY, FILL MY GLASS!"

It was midday, and Major Acland was having a meal with another officer. They sat under a shady tree at a makeshift table, eating cold roast beef and washing it down with wine. Nathaniel had been watering the major's horse when the other officer called to him. Nathaniel looked at the man. He was fat, and his nose was almost the same color as his scarlet coat.

"The boy's not your servant," Major Acland said.

"Stuff and nonsense," the fat officer said. "Americans are all natural-born servants. Aren't you, boy?"

"Yes, sir," Nathaniel said as he poured wine in the man's glass. Inside, he burned with anger. But by waiting on the man, he could overhear their conversation.

"The rebels are more clever than we thought they would be," Major Acland said. "Our scouts have spotted fortifications to the south. They are very well built. It appears that the road to Albany is blocked."

"The solution is clear," the fat officer said. "Outflank 'em! Rush around the fort and attack from the rear. Those rebels are no match for British powder and steel, fort or no fort." The man belched, then tossed the wine down his throat. Nathaniel glanced at Major Acland. He was stroking his chin thoughtfully.

"Yes," Acland drawled. "Let us hope it will be that easy."

THE SEARCH PARTY RETURNED to camp at nightfall. Nathaniel flopped down outside his tent. He looked down at his aching feet. His shoes were nearly worn through.

"How was the march?" asked a voice. Nathaniel looked up and saw Ben Freeman smiling at him.

"Tiring," Nathaniel replied. "I won't be able to walk another mile for at least a week."

"We'll see about that." Ben laughed.

Sure enough, the next day the tents were taken down and the British army was on the move once again.

Nathaniel's feet began to bleed as he plodded over the rough ground, but he knew he would have to bear it. General Burgoyne had given strict orders that none of the camp followers were to ride in the carts. Besides, Nathaniel wasn't about to ride in the carts. He was practically a soldier!

A few hours after they had set up camp, Nathaniel sat under a shady tree to rest. Just then, an officer strode to the center of camp and tacked a sheet of paper to a tree. Nathaniel and Ben went to read the paper. "It's an order from General Burgoyne," Nathaniel said. He began to read: "'The life of the soldier is the property of the king. And since neither friendly warnings, repeated requests, nor punishment have had any effect, the first soldier caught beyond the army sentinels will be instantly hanged.'"

Nathaniel shivered. "Are they including camp followers in that order, too?" he wondered.

"I don't know," Ben replied.

"Well, no matter how hungry or restless I

might be, I'll never step outside the camp again without permission," Nathaniel declared.

Ben smiled at his friend. "*You're* going to follow orders? We'll see about that, Nathaniel Phillips," he said.

CHAPTER FOUR
"This Victory Was Dearly Bought"

Nathaniel woke at dawn the next day. His legs ached, and his feet were so sore he could hardly stand. Nathaniel left the tent. The morning had dawned foggy and cold. A messenger galloped into the camp.

"The rebels have been spotted," he cried. All around Nathaniel, soldiers gathered excitedly to hear the news. Ben appeared at Nathaniel's side.

"This could be the battle we've been

expecting," he said.

"Ben!" yelled a voice. Nathaniel saw Captain Marshall on horseback, calling to his servant. "I am leading a section of General Fraser's army," Marshall said. "We are to march to the right and make a wide sweep behind the Americans. Follow closely behind. I may need to send messages to General Burgoyne's army at the center of battle."

"Yes, sir!" Ben called, and Marshall joined his troops.

"I'd give anything to see that battle," Nathaniel said, tagging along with Ben. "I'm coming with you."

Ben hesitated. "That may not be a good idea."

"I'm not afraid," Nathaniel told him stubbornly. "I can make myself useful by fetching water and helping the wounded."

Ben shrugged his shoulders. "Suit yourself," he said. "But don't say I didn't warn you."

The sun broke through the clouds. General Burgoyne confidently led his huge army of six thousand troops from camp. Ben and Nathaniel followed Fraser's army of more than two thousand, which broke off from the main group and marched off to the right. Nathaniel saw Captain Marshall on horseback leading his troops. He seemed invincible in his bright red uniform.

Nathaniel's legs felt weak as he marched with the army mile after mile up a steep slope. At last they reached the top. Nathaniel could see a large, cleared patch of farmland surrounded by a dense wood.

"Where do you suppose the rebels are now?" Nathaniel wondered out loud. "Do you think they have all turned tail and fled, Ben?" he asked. But his friend had disappeared.

"Ben?" Nathaniel said, looking around. "Ben!" he called more loudly. He saw Ben disappear into the woods off to the right, as

General Fraser's troops marched into the field. Ben was deserting. He could be hanged!

Horrified, Nathaniel pushed through the lines of troops and ran into the woods. As he moved blindly through the trees, branches scratched at his face and arms. He continued to shout Ben's name.

Nathaniel's ears filled with a deafening roar. He fell to the ground, his hands to his ears. The woods had erupted in a flash of deadly rifle fire.

Just then, someone pulled him to his feet and gave him a rough push toward the nearest tree. Nathaniel looked back. Ben stood behind him.

"Climb!" Ben ordered.

Without a word, Nathaniel obeyed. He'd climbed many trees in his life, but none so fast as that orange-leaved maple. Ben was right behind him.

Nathaniel pulled himself onto a thick

branch as shots rang out from the surrounding trees and the ground below.

"I reckon we'll be safe enough here," Ben said.

Nathaniel gazed through the branches. From where they were perched, he and Ben could see the open field where Fraser's troops had marched. Now his troops were scattering in fear, as rifle shots cracked all around them. "Where are the rebels?" Nathaniel asked, turning to Ben. Then he gasped. In the branches of the tree next to them, Nathaniel saw the long barrel of a rifle and a man in a billowy, butter-colored shirt behind it.

"That's one of Colonel Dan Morgan's men," Ben whispered. "They're American riflemen, the best shots in the world. They learned to fight frontier-style in the French and Indian War, shooting at the enemy from the cover of trees and bushes."

Now the soldier was aiming his rifle into the group of British soldiers that had emerged from the woods. Nathaniel watched, his heart pounding, as the rifleman pulled the trigger. Instantly, an officer collapsed on the ground.

Nathaniel gasped. "'Tis Captain Marshall!" he whispered hoarsely to Ben. "We have to do something!"

"Too late," Ben said grimly. "Good Captain Marshall has been shot."

By now, more blazes of rifle fire were erupting from the trees.

"They're aiming for officers," Ben whispered. "The regular soldiers often flee without men to lead them."

"We must do something!" Nathaniel moaned.

"What?" Ben replied. "We have no weapons. We can do nothing but watch and wait."

Nathaniel gazed out at the field. The British soldiers tried to fire back, but their muskets could not fire as far as the rebels' rifles. Besides, the Americans were well hidden in the trees. Before long, dozens of British officers and soldiers were lying dead or wounded. The remaining troops began to retreat.

"We've got them now, boys!" called a voice from a nearby tree. Whooping and shouting, the rebels in their blousy, fringed shirts and coonskin caps began to drop from the trees. They charged into the clearing, waving their rifles.

Nathaniel immediately tried to jump to the ground. "We have to go after them!" he cried.

"Wait, Nathaniel!" Ben called. "Look!"

Nathaniel gazed through the trees. General Burgoyne and his army had reached the clearing. The brash Americans were outnumbered.

"Hurrah!" Nathaniel shouted. "The rebels will pay for their evil deeds now!"

General Burgoyne's army began to drive the riflemen back. The Americans scattered and ran for the woods; musket fire rained around their heads.

As the Americans disappeared into the woods, Nathaniel heard a strange noise. "'Tis a turkey gobble," he said to Ben, puzzled.

"Colonel Morgan is signaling his men," Ben told him. "He has a small instrument that woodsmen use to imitate a turkey's call."

"How do you know so much about the riflemen?" Nathaniel asked.

Ben shrugged. "I've heard talk of Colonel Morgan," he said. "He is a hero on the frontier."

"That must be him," Nathaniel said, nodding toward a tall man on the edge of woods. The man looked very angry.

By Colonel Morgan's second turkey call, the riflemen had regrouped. They emerged from the trees again, this time more slowly. Almost at the same time, American troops charged in from the left.

The Americans were led by a short, muscular man on a fine brown horse. "Come on, boys!" he called, waving his men on. "Hurry up, my brave boys!" The man hurled line after line of troops against the startled British.

"Who is that?" Nathaniel asked.

"General Benedict Arnold," Ben replied. "He's a powerful fine fighter. 'Tis said the Americans will follow him anywhere."

Nathaniel watched in horror as the deadly battle raged between Burgoyne's army and the rebels. For a time it seemed that the rebels were gaining. Then a group of German soldiers arrived with four cannon. Nathaniel recognized the Germans as part of General Burgoyne's forces. They set the cannon near the top of the hill and aimed them at the Americans.

Cannon fire boomed over the musket and rifle fire, and echoed through the woods. Nathaniel steadied himself on the branch while the fierce fighting continued.

The rifle fire from the surrounding trees

grew louder and more frequent. Colonel Morgan's men had stationed themselves once again in the trees and bushes. Nathaniel saw that they had found new targets: the British officers and soldiers manning the cannon. They began to fall in dead and wounded heaps, and the great guns were silenced.

When the British were driven back across the field, the rebels seized the cannon. They tried to turn the guns on the British, but Burgoyne's army came charging back with bayonets. The Americans headed back for the woods, regrouped, and charged again. Nathaniel counted six charges and counter-charges, as the number of dead and wounded soldiers grew ever higher.

Nathaniel felt like crying when he saw the number of gallant men who fell on both sides. The rich farmland was stained red with blood. General Burgoyne had been wrong about the enemy, Nathaniel decided. The Americans were not as organized or experienced as the British soldiers, but they fought with courage, determination, and cunning.

Darkness fell and the battle slowed. Regiment by regiment, the rebels began to withdraw. The riflemen faded back into the trees. The exhausted British army remained in the smoky clearing, huddled in small groups among the dead and wounded.

"The rebels have left the field," Nathaniel said. "Does that not mean the British have won the battle?"

"Perhaps," Ben said slowly. "But General Burgoyne has lost men he cannot replace." Ben climbed down from the tree and Nathaniel followed. "This victory was dearly bought," Ben said.

NATHANIEL WAS ALMOST SICK as he and Ben picked their way through the battlefield. More than six hundred bodies were scattered on the open field. The moans of the wounded lingered in Nathaniel's ears after he had left the field to return to the British camp.

Walking through the chilly gloom, Nathaniel and Ben passed a group of grim-faced camp followers. The women were heading for the battlefield.

"Where are they going?" Nathaniel asked.

"To strip the dead," Ben said in a quiet voice. "Dead men have no need for shoes; live men do."

The two boys moved silently down the road where, only hours before, the proud British army had marched. After a two-mile hike, they reached the camp. A guard snapped to attention and pointed his musket at them. "Who goes there?" he called.

"Captain Marshall's servants," Ben called back.

The guard lowered his musket. The boys entered the camp, where fires were already burning. A man turned to the boys as they passed by in the darkness. "Are you not

Captain Marshall's orderly?" he asked Ben.

"I am," Ben replied. "Or rather, I was."

The soldier turned back to the fire. "He was a brave man," the soldier said.

Ben stopped. Nathaniel thought he saw tears in his friend's eyes. Nathaniel didn't know what to say. He had never thought of men who fell in battle as *men*, only soldiers. Now, there was no comfort he could give to Ben, who had been Captain Marshall's loyal servant.

Later, while they lay on the ground among a group of dozing soldiers, Nathaniel turned to his friend. "Ben?" he whispered hesitantly.

"What is it?" Ben asked.

"Were you trying to desert when you ran into the woods today?" Nathaniel asked.

"No," Ben said. "I promise you, I wasn't deserting. Good night, Nathaniel."

"Good night," Nathaniel said. He shut his eyes tight and tried to will himself to sleep, but it was no use. The cries and moans of the wounded men nearby were too much to bear.

In the distance, Nathaniel heard the howling of wolves. They, too, would visit the dead on the battlefield.

It would be a very long night.

CHAPTER FIVE
"One Move and You're Dead!"

Nathaniel dragged himself up the river-bank, lugging two heavy buckets filled with water. The cold water kept spilling on his nearly bare legs, chilling him to the bone.

He gritted his teeth and continued back up the hill, through the woods, and into the British camp.

It was just after sundown on the sixth of October, almost three weeks after the battle. General Burgoyne and his men had continued to hold the field where they had won their bitter victory, but the American army still blocked the road to Albany. The British would eventually have to fight their way past the rebels or return to Canada in defeat.

Nathaniel's shoes had long since worn out, and his bare feet had grown rough and calloused. He could not begin to count how many trips he'd made to the river in the past two weeks. The army needed water for more than just cooking and washing. A constant supply of water was needed to ease the suffering of the wounded soldiers.

When Nathaniel entered the camp he tried to block his ears against the cries of the men lying upon the ground. Some were wrapped only in blood-stained blankets.

"Give us some water, lad," one of them called, and reached out a bandaged arm. "Have mercy on a dying man!"

Nathaniel stopped and poured a bit of water into the soldier's dented tin cup.

"Good lad," said a voice behind him.

Nathaniel turned and saw Major Acland standing beside a tent. His left arm was in a bloody sling. "The men have scarce comfort," he said sadly. "I thank you for your help."

"You're welcome, sir," Nathaniel said with modesty. "Would you care for some water?"

"Thank you," the major said. He came to Nathaniel with a tin cup, which he dipped into the bucket.

"Tell me, sir," Nathaniel said. "How long will we remain here?"

Acland looked at Nathaniel with suspicion. "You're not thinking of deserting, are you, Phillips?"

"Oh, no, sir," Nathaniel said. "But it seems to me that we are helpless here. Why don't we go forward? Why don't we retreat?"

Major Acland smiled wryly.

"You sound like General Burgoyne himself," Acland said. "We had a council of war yesterday. The good general insisted that we move forward. 'Tis madness, though," he said bitterly. "Unless we get help from troops in New York City, we are unlikely to defeat the rebels."

"Then are we to wait here and starve?" Nathaniel asked.

Acland smiled and rubbed Nathaniel's head. "Don't worry, lad," he said. "Tomorrow Gentlemen Johnny himself is leading a party to forage for supplies. Fifteen hundred of our troops will harvest the crops of nearby farms. And they will see just exactly where our rebel friends are hiding." With that, Major Acland turned and entered his tent.

Nathaniel continued on his way with the buckets. He did not stop until he had reached Mistress Dargin's tent. Mistress Dargin was outside with several other ladies, washing bandages in an iron pot filled with boiling water.

"There you are, Nathaniel," she said, pushing her red hair from her eyes. "Set the buckets down next to the fire now; that's a good lad."

"Yes, ma'am," Nathaniel said.

Mistress Dargin looked at him kindly. "You look a bit pale," she said. "Why don't you sit down and take something to eat? There's a scrap of firecake left in the pan, I think."

Grateful, Nathaniel dropped down on his knees next to the fire.

"Well, I don't see what our Gentleman Johnny is waiting for," a woman was complaining. "Why doesn't he just attack the rebels and be done with it? Our army grows weaker every day, with more men dyin' and the animals half-starved."

"We're half-starved as well, while Burgoyne makes merry with his officers and his lady friend," another woman put in.

"The general must know what's best," Mistress Dargin replied as she lifted a long bandage out of the steaming pot with a forked stick.

Nathaniel stared down at the thin firecake in his bowl. The women were right to complain, he thought. It seemed that all he ate these days were these thin, burned circles of flour, washed down with rum and dirty water. There was little other food to be had. A few days earlier, a group of soldiers and women had wandered outside camp to dig potatoes in a nearby field. An American patrol had surprised them and opened fire, shot fourteen, and took the others prisoner. Still, sometimes a soldier brought back a rabbit or pheasant from the woods. That was a rare treat, since anyone who stepped outside the camp risked death.

Nathaniel was raising the cake to his mouth when a ragged-looking soldier appeared beside him.

"I'll take that, boy," the soldier said. "You don't look like you're very hungry, anyway."

Nathaniel looked up at the soldier. It was the second time in two days that someone had tried to steal his food.

"I'm hungry enough," Nathaniel said. But when he tried to stuff the firecake into his mouth, Nathaniel felt the sharp tip of a bayonet pressed to his back.

"I said, hand it here," the soldier growled. "A fighting soldier needs more food than a stripling."

Nathaniel reluctantly gave the man his bowl, and the pressure on his back disappeared. Nathaniel looked down, fighting back tears.

"Here," said a familiar voice. Nathaniel looked up. Ben stood beside him, his bowl in hand. "You can have some of mine, if you'd like." He tore his own firecake in two and handed half to Nathaniel. "You've been looking mighty poorly of late."

"I'm fine, thank you," Nathaniel said crossly. "You needn't give me your charity."

"Don't be silly," Ben said. "Take it, or you'll starve. Then I'll have no friends in this camp." Nathaniel reluctantly accepted the food.

"I'll pay you back once we've got new supplies," Nathaniel said as he gobbled down the firecake.

"Don't fool yourself," Ben said sharply. "We're cut off here. There will be no new supplies."

"But the army is going to gather crops," Nathaniel said. "Gentleman Johnny himself is leading fifteen hundred troops to forage tomorrow."

Ben looked at Nathaniel through narrowed eyes. "Aye," he said. "I've heard those rumors, too."

"'Tis no mere rumor," Nathaniel insisted. "I learned it from Major Acland. He was at the council of war where the plan was made."

Ben looked thoughtful, then smiled at Nathaniel. "Well, that's tomorrow. In the meantime, I could use some more food. Come on." With that, he got to his feet and walked off. Nathaniel followed.

"Where are we going?" Nathaniel asked, as his friend headed out of camp and toward the woods. "We mustn't leave the camp, or the general will have us executed."

"Shh," Ben said. He led Nathaniel through the woods. The only noise they made was the crackling of flame-red leaves under their feet. After a few minutes, Ben stopped. He pointed through the trees to a small clearing overgrown with weeds. "We'll get potatoes in that field," he whispered. "You don't want to die of starvation, do you?"

"No," Nathaniel said. At the very thought of food, the gnawing pains in his stomach grew sharper. "But we'll have to be quick. If there are rebel soldiers patrolling nearby, they might shoot us. Maybe if we put just a few potatoes under our shirts and run right back to camp. . ."

"Fair enough," said Ben. "Let's go!"

They ran toward the clearing. Halfway to

the small field, Nathaniel tripped over a tree root and landed flat on his stomach. He gasped. He had knocked the breath out of himself.

Ben reached the field and began to dig through the dirt with his hands. He stopped and looked around when he realized Nathaniel had not made it to the clearing. "Nathaniel?" he called, looking around. "Hallo! Where are you, Nathaniel?"

"Over here," Nathaniel called back weakly. He struggled to his feet and Ben ran to his side.

"Are you all right?" Ben asked.

"I'm fine," Nathaniel replied, brushing himself off. He was about to say more when there was a rustle in the bushes behind them. "What's that?" he asked. "A bear?"

Ben glanced around at the trees. "Or a wolf, maybe," he said.

Just then, they heard the sharp click of a rifle being cocked. "You two, hold it right there," a voice boomed. "One move, and you're dead!"

Nathaniel shook so hard that he was sure the man with the rifle would think he was moving. He and Ben were about to be shot by an American patrol!

CHAPTER SIX
"They Could Be Deciding the Outcome of This War"

Nathaniel and Ben froze as the soldier steadied his rifle. By the light of the moon, Nathaniel could see that the large man was one of Colonel Morgan's riflemen.

"What are you doing out here?" the man demanded.

"I'm Ben Freeman," Ben told him. "And this is Nathaniel Phillips. We carry information from Burgoyne's camp."

The rifleman's eyes narrowed. "From Burgoyne, eh?" he said.

"General Arnold knows of me, sir," Ben added.

Nathaniel looked at Ben with terror. Why was Ben pretending they were spies for the Americans? Surely they would be in even worse trouble when it was discovered they had lied.

A sudden chill ran down Nathaniel's spine. Could Ben be telling the truth? he wondered. Was it possible that his friend was a spy?

"All right, move along," the rifleman said gruffly. "I'm taking you back to camp. And not a word out of you," he added, glancing around at the trees, "or I'll send you both to meet your Maker."

The large man gestured with his rifle that they should walk in front of him through the woods.

"Say nothing," Ben whispered to Nathaniel. "It's safer for you that way. I'll do the talking."

Nathaniel gave a slight nod to show that he had heard. Then they began to make their way silently through the woods. A few times, the man moved ahead of the boys to clear a path, but he kept his rifle constantly pointed at them.

Nathaniel wondered what would become of Ben and himself when they reached the American camp. Would General Arnold think they were British spies? Nathaniel knew what happened to spies. More often than not, they were strung up on the nearest tree.

An owl hooted in the distance, and Nathaniel was sure he heard the faint howl of a wolf. At least the American has a rifle, Nathaniel told himself.

Finally, after a very long walk, he saw campfires burning in the distance. His heart raced. They were nearing the rebel camp.

"Who goes there?" a guard called.

"Timothy Murphy," the rifleman replied.

"I've brought two lads from Burgoyne's camp as well."

The guard stepped aside, and Timothy Murphy nudged the boys with his rifle. "Step lively," he said.

The American camp was quiet as they approached. Timothy Murphy led Nathaniel and Ben to one of the larger tents. "Wait here," he said. "And don't try to run if you value your lives."

Nathaniel looked around the camp. He was surprised to see it was very much like the British camp. It had the same campfires, the same tents, and the same weary but determined-looking soldiers.

A moment later, Timothy Murphy came out of the tent, followed by a young American officer. The officer looked sharply at the two boys, then turned back to the rifleman. "General Arnold is meeting with his aides," he said. "He is not to be disturbed. If these boys hold any information of value, it can wait until tomorrow."

Timothy Murphy gave a short nod and disappeared somewhere into the camp. "Come along," the young officer said to Nathaniel and Ben. "You will spend the night with the other prisoners."

Nathaniel and Ben followed the officer to a heavily guarded group of tents set apart from the rest of the camp. "In there," the officer said, and jerked his head toward one of the tents.

The two boys entered it and stumbled in the darkness over sleeping bodies. There were a few angry protests; one man reached out and cuffed Nathaniel on the leg. Finally, Ben pulled Nathaniel toward a spot near the back of the tent.

"Don't worry," he whispered. "We'll be all right."

"But what—?" Nathaniel began.

"Shh!" Ben said. "Someone will hear you. Must you always be asking so many questions? Remember, Nathaniel, say nothing to anyone."

Nathaniel drew his knees up to his chest and buried his face in his arms. He was trying to be brave, but he had no idea what the next day would bring. He, Nathaniel Phillips, was now a prisoner in the American camp. What would be his fate if Ben was lying about having information for General Arnold?

Nathaniel leaned back against the wall of the tent, certain that he would never fall asleep. Ben was already snoring beside him.

Nathaniel huddled in the darkness and tried not to think about the grave danger they were in. He dreaded the morning.

NATHANIEL SAT UP with a start. Sunlight filtered through the tent. He must have fallen asleep after all. The other prisoners were being roused for breakfast.

Nathaniel turned to see whether Ben was awake. His stomach sank. His friend was no longer beside him.

Alarmed, Nathaniel asked one of the prisoners what had become of the older black boy. The prisoner, a German soldier with a big moustache, merely shook his head.

"Heinrich does not speak English, I am afraid," another prisoner said. He held a pet raccoon on his lap. "I have seen your young friend. The Americans took him away at daybreak."

And they will come for me next, Nathaniel thought with a shudder.

Just then, a soldier entered the tent. "You there!" he called, looking straight at Nathaniel. "Come with me."

The German prisoner who spoke English patted Nathaniel on the shoulder. "Goodbye, my friend," he said.

Nathaniel stepped out of the tent. He broke into a cold sweat and his knees buckled. A group of soldiers were throwing a noose over the branch of a nearby tree.

I must be brave, Nathaniel told himself.
He knew they were going to hang him. He
must be brave, like a soldier.

He looked up at the young officer who
had called him from the tent. Relief flooded
Nathaniel's heart. The young officer was
smiling at him! "Please accept our apologies
for last night, Master Phillips," he said.

Apologies? Nathaniel nodded, dazed.

"I'm sure you understand," the officer
went on, "that we can't be too careful these
days, with the enemy so near."

"Yes, sir," Nathaniel mumbled. Out of the
corner of his eye, Nathaniel could see a
ragged-looking soldier being pushed toward
the hanging tree.

The rope wasn't for Nathaniel after all.
"Who is to be hanged?" Nathaniel asked.

"A British messenger," the officer said.
"Poor devil, he was caught trying to sneak
past our troops. He carried information for
Burgoyne's army. Some British troops are

traveling north from New York."

"They have come to save Burgoyne?" Nathaniel asked.

"Hardly," the young officer said. "But they have sent sixty ships upriver. That could force us to divert some of our forces. That, along with the information you brought, has made our course clear."

Nathaniel's head was swimming. Information he had brought? What could that be?

By now, the officer had left Nathaniel by a large tent in the middle of camp. Ben stood outside the tent.

"Ben!" Nathaniel cried.

"Shh," Ben said. "I want to hear what's being said."

"What's going on?" Nathaniel asked, joining his friend outside the tent.

"They could be deciding the outcome of this war," Ben said. "Listen."

"Our spies tell us that Burgoyne has

brought fifteen hundred men to a nearby wheat field," a voice was saying inside the tent. "Some of the soldiers are to gather the unharvested wheat. It does not appear they are in a hurry to fight."

"The woods surrounding the wheat field provide an ideal position for Colonel Morgan and his riflemen," someone else said. "The British are offering you battle, General Gates."

"Well, then," a raspy voice replied, "order Colonel Morgan to begin the game."

"The riflemen alone are not enough, sir!" bellowed another voice. "You must send a stronger force."

"General Arnold, I have nothing for you to do," General Gates said sharply. "I have relieved you of your rank. You have no business here."

Nathaniel leaned closer to the tent. Someone said quickly, "I'm afraid General Arnold has a point, sir. You must support the riflemen."

There was a long silence. "All right," General Gates said finally. "I'll send out a brigade of eight hundred men to attack the British left flank. Morgan will attack their right. Arnold, you are dismissed."

Nathaniel and Ben jumped back from the tent as General Arnold stormed past them and walked away. Other officers rushed out and headed to their troops.

Nathaniel felt his heartbeat pounding in his ears. Another battle was about to begin.

"HOW COULD YOU?" Nathaniel glared at Ben. "How could you betray your friends?"

"The British are not my friends," Ben replied.

It was hours later. Nathaniel and Ben were in the American camp, watching line after line of troops march off to battle. Ben had told Nathaniel of his spying; how he had often snuck off to the American camp to report on British plans. In the distance, Nathaniel could hear the cracking of gun fire. The battle had begun.

"Do you hear that?" Nathaniel asked, as a distant cannon boomed. "That's your fault. All of this is happening because *you* told the rebels of the British army's plans!"

"Don't be a fool!" Ben snapped. "The battle was bound to happen. And the sooner it is done, the better."

"But what about your friends?" Nathaniel asked. "What about Captain Marshall?"

"I was very sorry for him," Ben said quietly. "But he was a soldier."

"And now he's dead," Nathaniel said.

"He's not alone," Ben replied, his eyes flashing with anger. "Don't you see? Captain Marshall fought and died because he was paid to be a soldier. Remember the sign—his life was the property of the king." Ben pointed to a group of American soldiers. "These men are fighting and dying for a cause. They are fighting for their freedom." Ben's voice was almost a whisper. "That's something worth fighting for."

A very confused Nathaniel sat next to Ben. Everything he thought he knew had been turned inside out. War was awful, not glorious. It was only worthwhile to fight for important things. And, in this war, could it be that the rebels had the better cause to fight for?

A group of soldiers suddenly gave a loud cheer. Nathaniel looked up and saw General Arnold on a fine brown horse, saluting the men. Arnold looked upset, Nathaniel thought. "He is anxious to lead his men into battle," Ben explained. "But General Gates, the commander, hates Arnold. He doesn't want Arnold to win any glory on the battle-field."

Nathaniel saw General Arnold stare past him and Ben. He turned to see what Arnold was looking at. An old, bald man in a general's uniform sat in a chair under a shade tree. Two other men sat beside him. Despite the roar of the distant battle, the men were laughing and talking.

"That's General Gates," Ben said. "He commands the American troops, but he has no stomach for battle." Gates looked up and noticed Arnold. The two generals stared at each other. Then Gates sneered and looked away.

General Arnold's face flushed bright red. He looked as if he would explode, Nathaniel thought. The general drew his sword and waved it over his head.

"Victory or death!" General Arnold roared. He dug his spurs into his rearing horse. The horse galloped off, carrying Benedict Arnold into battle.

CHAPTER SEVEN
"Victory or Death!"

General Arnold's cry echoed through the camp. "Victory or death!" men shouted as they scrambled to join the battle. General Gates got up from his chair and trotted over to Ben and Nathaniel. He cursed under his breath when he watched Arnold gallop off into battle.

"Major Armstrong!" he called back. "I need you immediately!"

"Yes, sir," said one of the men under the

tree, rushing up beside the general.

"I fear that hothead Arnold will do some rash thing," General Gates said. "You must tell him to use caution, before he leads us all into trouble."

"Right away, sir," Major Armstrong said. He quickly climbed on his horse and rode after Arnold.

"Just talking to Arnold may not be enough," Gates muttered, frowning. Then he spotted Nathaniel. "You, boy!" he said. "Catch up with Major Armstrong yonder. Tell him that I want General Arnold brought back immediately to my headquarters."

"Me, sir?" Nathaniel stammered.

"Make haste," General Gates snapped, "or the major will be gone."

Nathaniel took off at a run. "Major Armstrong!" he called as he drew close to the major. "Wait! I have a message from General Gates!"

But Armstrong did not hear Nathaniel.

He broke through the ranks of soldiers and turned his horse toward the battle.

Ben came alongside Nathaniel on a brown horse. "Get on!" Ben said. Nathaniel climbed behind Ben on the horse. Ben kicked the horse's ribs, and the two boys galloped for the battlefield.

Terror knotted Nathaniel's stomach as they drew near the gunfire. When they broke into a clearing, he saw that the battle was already raging. A brigade of Americans was attacking a group of British soldiers on a small hill above the wheat field. The Americans charged up the slope. The British delivered a heavy volley of musket fire and fired their cannon, but most of the shots flew harmlessly over the heads of the charging Americans.

The British then lowered their guns, pointed their bayonets, and charged at the Americans. Nathaniel cringed as the Americans fired their muskets at point-blank range. The scarlet line of British soldiers, who were advancing shoulder-to-shoulder, crumpled and fell.

Nathaniel tore his eyes away from the battle and looked for Major Armstrong. He spotted Colonel Morgan and his riflemen off to the left. Morgan's men were shooting at another wing of Burgoyne's army, which was posted behind a rail fence. Another group of American soldiers charged in from the other side, causing the British to scatter. Only the hired German soldiers in the center held their ground.

"Look!" Ben called, and pointed into the distance. Nathaniel saw Major Armstrong sitting on his horse under a tree. It didn't look as if he were eager to dash onto the field.

"We'll catch him now," Nathaniel called. Ben turned their horse in Armstrong's direction.

Just then, General Benedict Arnold burst out of the forest onto the battlefield, galloping furiously on his large brown horse. Nathaniel saw Major Armstrong take off in hot pursuit.

General Arnold headed for a group of American soldiers in the middle of the battle. Nathaniel and Ben cut across the field toward them. Nathaniel prayed they wouldn't be caught by any bullets.

"Whose regiment is that?" Nathaniel heard General Arnold shout as they drew closer.

"Colonel Lattimer's, sir," one of the men replied.

"Ah! My old Norwich and New London friends," General Arnold cried over the roar of the battle. "God bless you! I'm glad to see you."

With that, he spurred his horse and continued his ride across the battlefield. Nathaniel bit his lip as Ben switched direction to intercept him. The general was certainly a hard man to follow.

The next brigade of Americans gave General Arnold a rousing cheer when he approached. Arnold placed himself at the head, waving his sword and shouting to the men.

Musket fire exploded all around them. Ben pulled back and led their horse to the edge of the woods.

"It looks as though General Arnold won't live long enough to receive General Gates's orders," he said.

Nathaniel watched in amazement as General Arnold led the soldiers in a charge up the hill. Gunfire continued to explode. Men dropped to the left and right of Arnold. When the others fell back, Arnold galloped back across the field toward Colonel Morgan.

"Colonel Morgan, that man over there on the gray horse is General Simon Fraser," Nathaniel heard him say. "He is rallying the enemy troops, and he must be disposed of."

Nathaniel's mouth dropped open. General

Fraser, he knew, was greatly loved by the British troops. "No!" he wanted to shout, but no words came out.

The riflemen began to fire at the British general. Nathaniel saw Timothy Murphy— the man who had brought him and Ben to the American camp—calmly climb a tree and settle himself in its branches. At the crack of Murphy's double-barreled rifle, General Fraser fell, and the British scrambled to retreat.

Nathaniel and Ben remained at the edge of the woods watching in awe. General Arnold charged all over the field, commanding regiment after regiment to storm the British. Everywhere he rode, American soldiers rallied, cheered, and threw themselves at the British. As Arnold rode across the battlefield, he left smoke and blood in his wake.

"We must stop him!" Nathaniel pleaded. Ben nodded and headed their horse toward the thick of the battle. They followed Arnold as he charged a small fort—a square of stacked logs—at the back of the battlefield. The fearless general drove his horse through an opening in the fort.

Just as he entered the fort, General Arnold was hit in the leg by a bullet. The next instant, his horse was shot out from under him. Arnold screamed in pain and fell to the ground, and his huge horse rolled onto Arnold's wounded leg.

American troops began streaming in after Arnold. The soldiers in the fort dropped their weapons in surrender. Nathaniel leapt from the horse and scrambled into the fort. Arnold was propped against the wall, his face twisted in agony. Nathaniel hurried toward him.

"No!" Arnold yelled. Nathaniel turned. An American soldier was about to stab the man who had shot Arnold. "Don't hurt him," Arnold said. "He's a fine fellow. He only did his duty."

At that moment, Major Armstrong strode

into the fort. He saluted Arnold. "General Arnold, sir," he called. "General Gates orders you back behind our lines!"

Arnold threw back his head and laughed. His face contorted in pain.

"The general has been shot," someone told Armstrong. Another officer leaned toward Arnold. "Where are you hit, sir?" he asked.

"In my leg," Arnold moaned. He gazed around. Dead and wounded soldiers were scattered on the grass. The gunfire of the waning battled crackled outside the fort. Nathaniel saw Arnold's face go deadly pale. "I wish it had been my heart," Arnold whispered.

NATHANIEL WANDERED through the battlefield. Ben was nowhere to be seen.

It was growing dark, and there would be no more fighting today. The Americans had won a great victory. General Burgoyne's army would never recover from the battle, Nathaniel thought. He tried to shut his eyes to the sight of the smoky field covered with bodies.

"You, there!" a soldier called to Nathaniel. "You'll be needed to assist in the hospital tent, boy. Wounded are being brought in by the score!"

Nathaniel nodded reluctantly. The last place he wanted to go was the hospital tent. He slowly headed to the large tent on the edge of the battlefield. As soon as he stepped through the flaps, he felt sick to his stomach. A number of operations were already in progress. He saw a doctor take a jagged, bloody saw and lean over a screaming soldier. The doctor put the saw to the soldier's wounded arm, and. . .

Nathaniel's head began to swim. Then the ground seemed to move, and everything went black.

CHAPTER EIGHT
"This War Is Not Yet Over"

The night air was cold, and the wind howled in the bare trees. Nathaniel shivered. He stood outside a tent. From within came the sounds of loud laughter and singing. The officers leading both the British and American armies were celebrating together. Earlier that day, October 17, 1777, General Burgoyne had surrendered to General Gates. The grand strategy to divide the colonies had utterly failed.

"Boy! More wine!"

Nathaniel looked up. A pair of men sat around a campfire. Nathaniel took a bottle from a nearby table and went to them. One wore the uniform of an American officer. The other man was a British major.

"I simply do not understand war," the British officer was saying.

"'Tis a bloody business," the American said, taking the bottle from Nathaniel.

"Bloody? 'Tis insane," the British major said. He nodded toward the distant tent, where a fresh chorus of singing could be heard. "Here we are making merry together, the best of friends. Only two weeks ago we were all doing our best to kill each other."

The American officer shook his head and gazed into the campfire. "It's an odd old world," he said sadly. "It's an odd old world."

"ANY NEWS OF GENERAL ARNOLD?" Nathaniel asked. It was past midnight. He and Ben were in a tent. Ben had been helping out in a hospital tent, while Nathaniel waited on the officers.

"He's mending better than expected," Ben said. "He refused to let the surgeon saw off his shattered leg." Ben chuckled. "He calls his doctors 'an ignorant set of pretenders.'"

Nathaniel smiled. "What will you do now that the campaign is over, Ben?" he asked.

Ben stared out into the cold, dark night.

"This war is not yet over. I'll continue with the American army," he said. "Perhaps they'll even let me do a bit of fighting now. What about you? Will you return to Canada?"

Nathaniel thought for a moment. Master Rodman's face flashed into his mind, and he shuddered. "I'll not go back north," he said. "I reckon I'll find my sister Polly. She lives near Albany, and will surely need help on the farm now that her husband is with the American army."

"Why don't you come with me?" Ben asked quietly. "A soldier's life can get powerfully lonely without a friend, and we'll see plenty more battles, no doubt."

Nathaniel shook his head. "I've seen enough fighting," he said. "You were right. 'Tis a terrible business." He hesitated. "You'll take care of yourself, won't you, Ben?"

Ben laughed as he headed out of the tent. "Don't I always?" he said. "Once the fighting is over, and we have won independence, I'll come and visit you on your peaceful farm. I give you my word." With that, Ben disappeared into the night.

Nathaniel leaned back on his blanket. He felt sad, yet hopeful, too.

He hoped that his friend would be able to keep his promise.

The Battle of Saratoga was a turning point in the Revolutionary War. It gave

Library of Congress

General John Burgoyne

Americans confidence that they could defeat the mighty British army. It also ended the British threat to take over New England.

After General Burgoyne surrendered, his soldiers were taken to Boston as prisoners of war. They were supposed to be sent to England, never to return to America. But the Americans realized that the return of those soldiers would allow England to send others to fight in their place. So the British prisoners from Saratoga were forced to march from Boston to Virginia the following

November. They stayed there until the war was over.

Probably the most important result of the battle was that the rest of the world saw that America could defeat the British. France decided to come into the war on the side of the Americans. With France's help, the colonies were finally able to win their independence from England in 1783.

More about . . .

Nathaniel, Ben, and Captain Marshall are fictional characters. But most of the other characters in the book are based on real people. Here is more about some of the major characters in the book.

General John Burgoyne, known to his friends and enemies as "Gentleman Johnny," was a very ambitious and confident man. Born penniless in 1722, he married into a wealthy family. Back then, rich men could buy positions in the British

In May 1775, Benedict Arnold led American forces in taking over Fort Ticonderoga, near Saratoga. This picture shows the Americans confronting the British leader at Fort Ticonderoga.

army. Burgoyne bought himself a high rank. He became a hero in the Seven Years' War and was a favorite of King George III. Burgoyne was tall and handsome, he liked to gamble, and he was popular with the ladies. He also wrote plays. After the war, the defeated general returned to London. He died in 1792.

Major John Dyke Acland was wounded at Saratoga and never fully recovered. The year after the battle, Acland was challenged to a duel after he loudly voiced his support for American independence. He survived the duel, but died of a heart attack shortly afterward.

General Horatio Gates, born in 1727, was a hero after the victory at Saratoga. He later commanded American forces in the South, but was badly defeated by the British at Camden, South Carolina, in 1780. General Gates looked and acted much older than his years. The common soldiers nicknamed him "Granny" Gates. He was a crafty leader and hated to take anyone's advice. Gates, who was very jealous of Benedict Arnold's popularity with the soldiers, died in 1806.

General Benedict Arnold, born in 1741, was a fiery, impulsive fighter. He lived for glory, and it was said he would lead men into battle anywhere.

Arnold was at the head of many winning

American armies during the early years of the war. But Arnold grew angry with American leaders. He thought they did not appreciate him. Arnold's wife was friends with a British officer named Major André. Arnold and André plotted to allow the British to take over West Point, an important fort on the Hudson River, in 1780. Their plot was discovered, and the Americans hanged Major André. Benedict Arnold escaped, joined the British army, and fought against his old comrades. He later sailed to England with his wife, and died there in 1801.

In America, the name "Benedict Arnold" has become synonymous with "traitor." But, by his own request, Benedict Arnold was buried in his American uniform.

Dan Morgan was born in 1736, and was a farmer on the frontier. At the age of twenty, Morgan volunteered to fight for the

Major André tried to smuggle the plans to West Point in the heel of his boot. This picture shows André and Benedict Arnold hatching their plot.

British in the French and Indian War. During the war, Morgan struck a British officer. He received five hundred lashes of the cat-o'-nine-tails as his punishment, and barely survived the harsh treatment.

Morgan's frontiersmen were considered the best troops in the American army during the Revolutionary War. After the war, Morgan returned to farming. He died in 1802.

African Americans, like Ben, served on

both sides during the war. They were soldiers, servants, and spies.

When the war began, slaves and freed blacks were not allowed in the American army. Then the British offered freedom to any slave who served in their army. Thousands of enslaved African Americans joined the British cause. In response, George Washington allowed African Americans to join the Continental Army.

Many Americans—especially slave owners—hated to give black people guns. They feared that black slaves might rise up against their owners. They were wrong. More than five thousand African Americans served as loyal and able soldiers in the American army.

During the War for Independence, many white Americans began to think that African Americans should enjoy freedom, too. In 1783—the year the war was won—Massachusetts became the first state to abolish slavery.

Camp Followers were with both American and British armies. In the 1700s, it was common for a small number of soldiers' wives to follow an army. These women were paid for cooking, nursing, and laundering. In addition to the wives, many other women would join the army as it traveled. Young children would come with their mothers on the army's march. Babies would be born between battles. No one knows for sure how many camp followers were with the armies, but it is known that armies usually had more camp followers at the end of a campaign than at the start.

Read These Books to Learn
More about the Revolutionary War . . .

Alderman, Clifford Lindsey, *Guns for General Washington.* [New York: Four Winds Press, 1974.]

Bokless, Katherine and John, *Spies of the Revolution.* [Philadelphia: Lippincott, 1962.]

Clinton, Susan, *The Story of the Green Mountain Boys.* [Chicago: Children's Press, 1987.]

Fradin, Dennis B., *The New York Colony.* [Chicago: Children's Press, 1988.]

Griffin, Judith Berry, *Phoebe and the General.* [New York: Coward, McCann & Geohegan, 1972.]

Tunis, Edwin, *Colonial Living.* [New York: Thomas J. Crowell Co., 1957.]

Other Books in the **STORIES OF THE STATES** series

American Dreams* by Lisa Banim

East Side Story*
Golden Quest*
by Bonnie Bader

Fire in the Valley
Mr. Peale's Bones
Voyage of the Half Moon*
by Tracey West

Forbidden Friendship
by Judy Eichler Weber

Children of Flight Pedro Pan
by Maria Armengol Acierno

A Message for General Washington
by Vivian Schurfranz

*Available in paperback

If you are interested in ordering other **STORIES OF THE STATES** books, please call Silver Moon Press at our **toll free** number (800) 874-3320 for ordering information.